THE HIDDEN PICTURE BOOK OF

AESOP'S FABLES

BOYDS MILLS PRESS

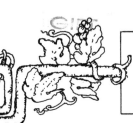

WHO WAS AESOP?

Legend tells us that Aesop lived in ancient Greece, about 600 B.C. It is often said that he was a slave, perhaps in some way misshapen.

The facts may be different. Maybe there was no single author of all the wonderful tales we call "Aesop's Fables." Maybe Aesop was the name of the person who first collected them. Or maybe Aesop was indeed a slave, who told the stories so well that he made them his own. His listeners followed him into his world of talking beasts, and they laughed to find them all so very human.

Now it's your turn to find the fun and wisdom in the world of Aesop (whoever he may have been). And just for you, there's more to find in the pictures. . . .

BELLING THE CAT

radish, candle, clothespin, golf club, ice-cream pop, paintbrush, paper clip, saltshaker, scrub brush, spatula, toothbrush, pencil

The mice were in big trouble—as big as a fat black cat. So they called a meeting.

"I can live with the terrible racket he makes when he's yowling at the moon," said one.

"Or the disgusting *slurp-slurp-slurp* when he's drinking his milk," said a second.

"But what will be the death of us," said the wisest old mouse, "is his silence."

It was true. When the cat felt like a snack and stalked the juicy little mice, he didn't make a sound.

"If only we weren't such tasty morsels," said a youngster.

"If only we could hear him coming," said another.

"I've got it!" cried a sharp-whiskered fellow. "Let's tie a bell around Master Cat's fat neck. Then *jingle-jingle-jingle*—we'll hear him coming a mile off."

What squeaks of approval! Right then and there the mice found an old bell, tied a ribbon on it, and crept up to the attic where the cat was snoozing. Only one thing remained to be done.

"And who," asked the wisest old mouse, "is going to tie the bell around Master Cat's neck?"

The mice's glances went from one to the other. They were in big trouble.

THE MORAL OF THIS STORY IS: SOME THINGS ARE EASIER TO SAY THAN TO DO.

THE FOX AND THE GRAPES

apple core, baseball mit, bird, cap, horseshoe, chisel, nail, shoe, snake, whale, butterfly

Fox was on the prowl one day when he spied some fine ripe grapes up above him.

"Oh, how plump and sweet and juicy," thought Fox. "Those I must have!" And with his great mouth watering, he leaped up to snatch a bunch.

But his razor-sharp teeth closed on air. He hadn't leaped quite high enough.

So he leaped again. And again. He leaped at this bunch and at that. He leaped as high as his strong back legs could thrust him, straining for the purple clusters.

But always they were just out of reach. Always as he fell back down, his mouth was still empty. And at last he was just too tired to jump anymore.

"Oh well," he told himself, "who cares? I can see now that those grapes aren't ripe—they're sour. Very sour. Not good enough for me."

And with that he stuck his nose in the air and went on his prowling way.

THE MORAL OF THIS STORY IS: IT'S EASY TO SAY YOU DON'T WANT WHAT YOU CAN'T HAVE.

THE CROW AND THE PITCHER

bell, book, mug, light bulb, mitten, paintbrush, ball-point pen, pencil, airplane, shoe,
piece of pie, closed umbrella

Crow was so thirsty. As she flapped on through the hot, dusty air she couldn't see a single drop down below to drink. The water in the well was far too deep for her. But something glinted at the side of the well—water in a pitcher! Down she dived and plunged in her beak.

What a disappointment. The water came only a little way up the pitcher, and her beak couldn't reach it. Poor Crow. She stretched all the way from her claws to the tip of her glossy black head. But the pitcher was narrow, and she couldn't get her head into it. She thrust her beak in from the right side, from the left side, from the front, from the back. Nothing brought her closer to the water.

Most creatures would have given up. But Crow was a persistent bird, a bird of intelligence, and she was very, very thirsty. She was determined to solve her problem.

Her eye fell on the pebbles all around and she had the answer. One by one she picked up the cleanest pebbles and plopped them into the pitcher. With every pebble the level of the water in the pitcher rose, until it reached the top. Daintily Crow dipped in her beak and drank her fill.

THE MORAL OF THIS STORY IS: NEED SOMETHING BADLY ENOUGH AND YOU'LL INVENT A WAY TO GET IT.

THE LION AND THE MOUSE

acorn, teacup, golf club, ice-cream pop, jump rope, milk carton, musical note,
artist's paintbrush, fountain pen, pushpin, wrench, glove

Mouse was scrambling over a sandy-colored rock when—
what was that?—it moved! A giant paw crashed down and caged
him inside steel claws. He had been scampering over Lion!

Now Lion lifted Mouse to his gaping mouth.

"No!" Mouse managed to squeak out. "Listen, Lion, I'm
sorry. I didn't mean to be rude. If you forgive me just this once,
I promise you won't regret it."

Lion lifted an eyebrow at this bold little creature.

"Lion," Mouse persuaded, "you can never have too many
friends. You never know when you might need one."

Lion roared—with laughter. "That's rich, my little friend," he
said. "But don't let me see you around here again." And with
that he set Mouse down and tapped him on his way.

As luck would have it, Mouse one day had the chance to
make good his promise.

It started with roars in the distance. Roars of anger and
frustration this time. Mouse scurried closer. He saw his friend
Lion cruelly trapped in a hunter's net that drew tighter and
tighter around him as he struggled.

"Leave it to me!" cried fearless Mouse, jumping up on
heaving Lion. He gnawed away at the treacherous ropes, and
Lion was free.

**THE MORAL OF THIS STORY IS: EVEN THE
SMALLEST FRIEND CAN BE A BIG HELP.**

THE GOOSE THAT LAID THE GOLDEN EGGS

clarinet, crayon, mug, mallet, paintbrush, scrub brush, shovel, spoon, stapler, radish, pinwheel

Early one morning a farmer cried out to his wife, "Come and look! Our goose has laid a golden egg!"

And so it had—a big, heavy, gleaming egg of solid gold. "How beautiful," marveled the farmer.

"What a wonderful present from our goose," chortled his wife.

The next day there was another golden egg, as big and heavy and gleaming as the first. On the third day there was a third egg, and on the fourth day, a fourth. And so it continued, egg after egg after egg.

There were so many eggs that the farmer and his wife started selling them. And they bought themselves fine hats, fine watches, fine candlesticks—every fine thing that caught their fancy. And the more fine things they bought, the more fine things they wanted.

"I want these new fine things over here," said the farmer.

"I want those new fine things over there," said his wife.

"And we *need* all these new fine things," they told each other, "right NOW!"

So they cut their goose open to help themselves to all the golden eggs inside.

"But there are no golden eggs inside!" gasped the farmer.

"No," sobbed his wife, "and now there is no goose."

THE MORAL OF THIS STORY IS: GET GREEDY AND YOU'LL END UP WITH NOTHING.

THE TRAVELERS AND THE PLANE TREE

jump rope, apple core, ring, crown, cupcake, feather duster, fish, eyeglasses, ice-cream cone, pliers, paintbrush, spoon, tube of toothpaste

It was a scorching hot noon. The sun burned high in the sky. Perspiring and parched, two travelers dragged themselves up a hilly road. Their shoes kicked up clouds of dust as they struggled on.

At last the travelers reached a plane tree. It spread its leafy branches over the roadside, a screen against the sun's hot rays. The travelers sank down in its shade. They were almost cool as they ate their midday meal.

They relished their rest. But finally they had to be on their way.

One of the travelers looked up at the tree.

"Did you ever consider," he asked his companion, "what a useless tree the plane tree is? It doesn't bear fruit. It doesn't offer us anything useful at all."

If you had ears that listened to the trees, you would have heard the plane tree cry out in indignation.

"You ungrateful man!" the plane tree cried. "You were just about done for when you sank into my cool shade. I sheltered you. I refreshed you so that now you are ready to go on your way again. I did that for you! And there you stand, under my beautiful canopy, calling me useless!"

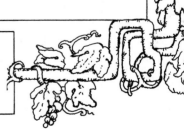

THE MORAL OF THIS STORY IS: PEOPLE OFTEN FORGET TO GIVE THANKS FOR WHAT'S DONE FOR THEM.

THE MILKMAID AND HER PAIL

book, carrot, fishhook, jar, key, sewing needle, paintbrush, spoon, aerosol can, toothbrush, wishbone, piece of pie

The farmer's daughter was a cheerful, hardworking girl. But how she loved to daydream! One morning she was up bright and early to milk the cow. Soon her pail was full to the brim. She settled it securely on her head and started back steadily toward the dairy. But her thoughts went skipping ahead.

"This creamy milk will make rich butter," she was thinking, "and I'll be able to sell the butter for plenty of money. With that money I'll buy a fine supply of eggs. And before you know it, the eggs will hatch into chickens. I'll sell the chickens and buy myself a truly elegant gown for the county fair!"

She laughed as she fancied the young fellows crowding around her. They were more real to her than the chickens clucking at her feet. She relished her future wealth. Scorning her suitors, she tossed her head . . .

. . . and the milk came crashing and splashing down all over the farmyard cobblestones. The cat leaped in for a creamy feast before it all trickled away between the cracks, along with the milkmaid's dreams.

THE MORAL OF THIS STORY IS: DON'T COUNT YOUR CHICKENS BEFORE THEY'VE HATCHED.

THE TORTOISE AND THE HARE

book, candle, flashlight, key, mitten, paintbrush, pencil, whistle, canoe, shovel, eyeglasses, nail

One summer afternoon, Tortoise heard Hare jeering at him yet again.

"Can you believe anyone could be so slow?" Hare demanded of his admiring friends. "Here am I, faster than the wind, and he's just an upside-down bucket!"

This time Hare went too far. Tortoise jutted out his head, stuck out his stubby legs, and lumbered toward the mocking gang.

"Hare, I challenge you to a race!"

Hare could hardly hear Tortoise above the laughter. He doubted his ears. But Tortoise insisted, and Hare found the challenge too funny to resist. So the race was on.

Hare was soon out of sight. But Tortoise plodded on.

Hare got to thinking how ridiculous it was to run so fast on such a hot afternoon when Tortoise was never ever going to catch up with him. He thought he might as well take a rest. But Tortoise plodded on.

Hare dozed off into a long, deep sleep. But Tortoise plodded on.

When the crowd at the finish line sighted Tortoise, their shouting woke up Hare. Hare streaked like lightning toward the tape. But Tortoise, comfortably in front, plodded under.

**THE MORAL OF THIS STORY IS:
SLOW BUT STEADY WINS THE RACE.**

THE DOG AND THE REFLECTION

apple core, bell, candle, cupcake, key, artist's paintbrush, ball-point pen, pencil, safety pin, shoe, spoon, crayon

Dog was trotting along with a large piece of meat in his mouth. Don't ask where he had found it or how he had made it his own. Dog always thought the biggest and the best was his by right. And he always kept an eye out to make sure nobody had anything bigger and better than he had.

As he crossed the bridge over a stream, he looked to see whether there was anything below that he ought to grab. There surely was! He saw a dog, much like himself, carrying what appeared to be an enormous hunk of meat.

Without a moment's thought, Dog plunged into the water, his jaws already open wide. His own meat went flying down into the stream as he sank his teeth into his rival's juicy treasure—and found himself with a mouthful of water and weeds.

For, of course, it was his own reflection that had aroused his envy. And Dog for once went hungry.

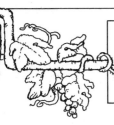

THE MORAL OF THIS STORY IS: GRAB ONLY FOR THE BIGGEST AND YOU COULD END UP WITH NOTHING.

THE CAT AND THE MICE

bicycle pump, ear of corn, hammer, loaf of bread, paintbrush, radish, screwdriver, sickle, shoe, toothbrush, tube of toothpaste, whistle

Mice, of course, are often in trouble. To begin with, all the cats in the world are after them.

The mice in this story had lived well for a while. The mistress of their big old house did not like cats. So the mice had grown fat and well rested, and their families were enormous.

A sneaky feline heard about this state of affairs. She made a pitiful appearance on the doorstep and purred her way into the mistress's favor. The cat loved nothing better than a greedy mouthful of mouse. Several times a day you could have seen her licking her whiskers after yet another feast.

The mice had a remedy. They stayed in their holes, venturing out only when they really needed to, and always with great care.

"Hmm," thought the cat. "I'll have to trick those mice into coming out again and getting careless." So she hung herself up by her hind legs on a peg in the kitchen. She kept perfectly still, pretending to be dead.

One of the bravest and smartest mice came out to investigate the silence. There was no fooling him. "You're very clever, Madam Cat," he cried. "But you won't catch us coming anywhere near you!"

THE MORAL OF THIS STORY IS: DON'T BE DECEIVED WHEN YOUR ENEMY PRETENDS TO BE HARMLESS.

THE BEAR AND THE TRAVELERS

carrot, magnifying glass, key, teacup, rocket, spoon, wrench, safety pin, radish, magic wand, fife, screw, ear of corn

Two travelers were walking through the woods. They had enjoyed many good times together and thought of themselves as friends.

Suddenly, one of the travelers spied a bear and scrambled up the nearest tree to safety.

The second traveler was less quick-sighted and nimble than his friend. But there was nothing slow about his thinking. As soon as he, too, saw the bear, he remembered hearing that bears leave corpses alone. He dropped to the ground and played dead.

He heard the bear coming toward him. The smell of the bear filled his nostrils. The claws of the bear struck the stones around him. The bear's fur brushed the second traveler's clothes and his skin. The bear's breath was hot on his face. The bear's wet nose snuffled at his ear. Tickling. Terrifying.

And then the bear lost interest, turned away, and was gone.

The first traveler had seen everything from his safe perch in the branches. Now that the peril had passed, he climbed down. He asked the second traveler what the bear had whispered.

"He told me," said the second traveler, "that I shouldn't travel with someone who deserts me in time of danger."

THE MORAL OF THIS STORY IS: WHEN DANGER STRIKES, YOU FIND OUT WHO YOUR FRIENDS ARE.

THE GOATHERD AND THE GOAT

bird, hairbrush, canoe, comb, crayon, football, ice-cream cone, artist's paintbrush,
ball-point pen, pencil, slice of bread, lollipop

The young goatherd was at his wits' end. It was evening, time to take his master's goats down from the hill. But one stubborn goat refused to come along.

The sun sank lower and lower in the sky. Soon it would be dark. What could the boy do? He couldn't leave the stubborn goat. But he must take the rest of the flock down to safety. Wolves roamed the hill in the night. Who knew what other dangers lurked in the shadows?

The stubborn goat *must* come with him. The goatherd pleaded. He bullied. He promised the goat a life with every blessing if only she would come down. But she would not.

It seemed to the boy that the stubborn goat was laughing at him. He was driven beyond reason. Before he knew what he was doing, he had snatched up a stone and thrown it at her.

The stone landed squarely on one of the goat's horns . . . and broke it off.

The boy ran over to the goat in dismay. He begged her not to tell his master what he had done.

"You silly boy," she said. "I won't need to tell the master anything. He will take one look at me, and my horn will tell him the whole story."

THE MORAL OF THIS STORY IS: IT'S NO USE TRYING TO HIDE SOMETHING THAT CAN'T BE HIDDEN.

COUNTRY MOUSE
AND CITY MOUSE

cap, record, candy bar, pencil, feather, ice-cream cone, battery, mallet, ladle, shoe,
yo-yo, magnifying glass

Country Mouse had a friend who lived in the city. One day he had a grand idea. He invited his friend to visit.

For every meal, Country Mouse happily set out roots that tasted richly of the earth. City Mouse didn't want to be hurtful, so he said, "Delicious." But after his third turnip stew, he had to add, "You really should come back with me, my friend, to sample the thousand treats in my pantry." And so he did.

Country Mouse squeaked with delight to see figs and dates and delicacies he'd never even heard of. City Mouse offered him a morsel of honey cake. But before Country Mouse could take it, City Mouse grabbed him and pulled him into a wretched little hole. Cook had come into the pantry.

Cook left at last and City Mouse persuaded Country Mouse that it was safe. Country Mouse had lost his taste for honey cake, but he was tempted by a cheese pie. He had his paw on it—but, once again, here came footsteps!

"It's the kitchen maid," whispered City Mouse as they hid. "She's leaving already."

"And so am I, good friend," said Country Mouse. "Thank you for inviting me. I'm glad you live so well. But I'm going back home for a nice nibble of rutabaga—in peace."

THE MORAL OF THIS STORY IS: FANCY PLEASURES WITH DANGER AREN'T WORTH SIMPLE PLEASURES WITH PEACE.

ANSWERS

Page 4

Page 6

Page 8

Page 10

Page 12

Page 14

Page 16

Page 18

Page 20

Page 22

Page 24

Page 26

Page 28

31

Copyright © 1995 by Boyds Mills Press
All rights reserved

Published by Bell Books
Boyds Mills Press, Inc.
A Highlights Company
815 Church Street
Honesdale, Pennsylvania 18431
Printed in the United States of America

Publisher Cataloging-in-Publication Data
San José, Christine.
The hidden picture book of Aesop's fables / by Christine San José ;
illustrated by Charles Jordan.—1st ed.
[32]p. : ill. ; cm.
Summary : Various objects are hidden within illustrations of Aesop's fables.
ISBN 1-56397-259-X
1. Picture puzzles—Juvenile literature. 2. Fables. [1. Picture puzzles.
2. Aesop's fables.] I. Jordan, Charles, ill. II. Aesop. III. Title.
398.2—dc20   1995
Library of Congress Catalog Card Number 94-71032   CIP

First edition, 1995
Book designed by Tim Gillner
The text of this book is set in 14-point Times Roman.
The illustrations are done in pen and ink.
Distributed by St. Martin's Press

10 9 8 7 6 5 4 3 2 1